Willis —

I thought you might enjoy
reading about an adventure in brass
as we set out on one of our own.

Dale

Braithwaite's Original Brass Band

Peter Stevenson

Frederick Warne
New York London

Frederick Warne & Company, Inc.
Printed in Singapore
for Frederick Warne & Company, Inc.
New York, New York

Library of Congress Cataloging in Publication Data

Stevenson, Peter, 1953-
    Braithwaite's original brass band
    SUMMARY: In an effort to recapture their music notes as they float
    up into space, the members of Braithwaite's Original Brass Band find
    themselves on a planet inhabited by a monster that collects the best
    bands in the world.
    [1. Bands (Music) – Fiction.   2. Music – Fiction.   3. Monsters – Fiction]
    I. Title
    PZ7.S848BR   E   80-18065
    ISBN 0-7232-6193-8

Braithwaite's Original Brass Band was the best band in all the land. The leader of the band, Ernest Braithwaite, came from a long line of bandleader Braithwaites that went way back to Great-Grandfather Ackroyd Braithwaite. He had founded the band so long ago that no one could remember exactly when.

For the past few weeks the members of
the band had thought of little else but the
Oswaldtwistle International Musical
Championship. They were determined to win,
especially Mr Braithwaite who liked to think
how proud Great-Grandfather Ackroyd would
have been.

On the morning of the Championship the five musicians were busy rehearsing. But no matter how hard they blew, no sound came out of their instruments. They blew and they blew — and still there was no music. The tuba player went red in the face. (It takes a lot of puff to play a tuba.) Something was terribly wrong. At that moment they looked up to see their music notes floating away in the sky.

"Follow those notes!" shouted Mr Braithwaite, and to his astonishment, they did. All five musicians took off into the air . . .

Up and up they flew, following their music notes.

"Keep going, lads," said Mr Braithwaite. "We must get our notes back or we'll have nothing to play at the Championship."

The tuba player felt airsick. The earth was getting smaller and smaller behind them.

Still they went on up and up . . . until they
found themselves in Outer Space. They
were heading straight for a small planet.
   "Perhaps we'll land there," said
Mr Braithwaite hopefully, and they did!

"Where are we?" the musicians cried, picking themselves up and dusting themselves down.

"And where are our music notes?" asked Mr Braithwaite.

They looked around . . . and saw hundreds and hundreds of toothy little monsters watching them.

"Take me to your leader," demanded
Mr Braithwaite bravely – and the little
monsters did exactly that. They led the
musicians to an important-looking red monster.
"I am the leader," he announced proudly,
waving a baton around his head. "You may call
me Maestro, the great conductor."

"I am a conductor too," said Mr Braithwaite,
"but we have lost our music notes. Have you
seen them anywhere?"

"Yes," said Maestro. "As a matter of fact,
I have stolen them." He pointed towards a
rickety old bandstand on which stood a strange
assortment of musicians. Maestro went on:
"I steal music from the best bands in the world.
When they come looking for their lost music,
I kidnap them."

"But why?" asked Mr Braithwaite twitching
his moustache. He could not help feeling
proud, even though he was annoyed.

"Ever since I was a young monster," Maestro
explained, "I have always wanted to be a
conductor. Now I can conduct the best bands
whenever I please."

With that he tapped his baton, raised his arms and began to conduct. The musicians started to play but they all played different tunes. The noise was . . .

. . . HORRIBLE!

Maestro was clearly enjoying himself, but
Mr Braithwaite was deafened by the noise.
"Quick, lads," he cried. "Grab some music
notes and escape while Maestro's busy
conducting. We must get home soon or we'll
be late for the Championship."
  So they all snatched a handful of notes and
crept silently away.

The band was almost out of sight when the
little red monsters realised what was
happening. Immediately, they set off in pursuit
of the five musicians.

"Oh dear, oh dear!" wailed the tuba player.
"How are we going to get home?"

"This way," said Mr Braithwaite, thinking fast. "Everyone down the music scale."

Suddenly they found themselves sliding down and down . . .

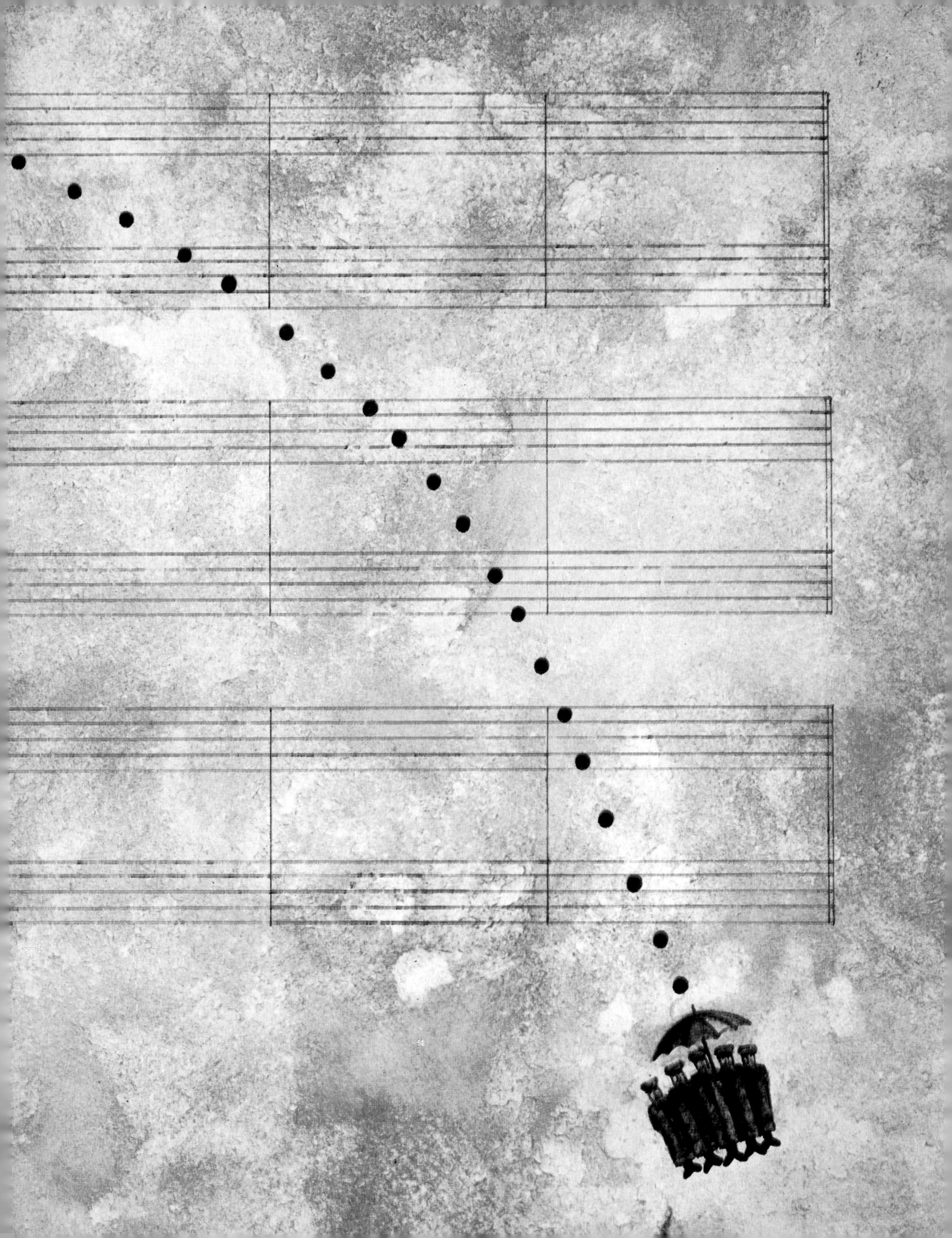

In no time at all the musicians were home.
Everything was ready for the Championship.
Or was it? In their rush to escape, they had
forgotten their instruments. How could they
possibly take part in the Championship now?

Then Mr Braithwaite remembered his Great-
Grandfather's old instruments in the attic.
"We can still win the Championship," he said.

And Braithwaite's Original Brass Band did win the Oswaldtwistle International Musical Championship. The five musicians played like they had never played before. The sound they made was quite out of this world for, after all, the notes they played had come from Outer Space! How proud Ernest Braithwaite was . . .

. . . And how proud Great-Grandfather Ackroyd would have been too!